CHRISTINE'S PICTURE BOOK

CHRISTINE'S PICTURE BOOK

HANS CHRISTIAN ANDERSEN
and Grandfather Drewsen

Footnotes and Postscript by Erik Dal
Translated by Brian Alderson

Holt, Rinehart and Winston
New York

First published in the United States in 1985 by
Holt, Rinehart and Winston, 383 Madison Avenue,
New York, New York 10017.
Published simultaneously in Canada by Holt, Rinehart and
Winston of Canada, Limited.

Library of Congress Cataloging in Publication Data
Main entry under title:

Christine's picture book.

1. Picture-books for children—Themes, motives.
I. Andersen, H. C. (Hans Christian), 1805–1875.
II. Drewsen, Adolph, 1803–1885.   III. Alderson, Brian.
NC965.C47   1985   741.64′2′094   85-5453

ISBN: 0-03-005729-9

First American Edition

Designer: Cherriwyn Magill
Printed in Italy

1 3 5 7 9 10 8 6 4 2

PREFACE

Members of the Stampe family in the garden at Nysø.
The children are Christine and her youngest sister Jeanina.
Oil painting by P.C. Skovgaard, 1865.

One day I found myself standing in the gardens of the Royal Library in Copenhagen with Christine Stampe's Picture Book in my arms. The library had kindly been taking care of the book for twelve years while my husband — whose property it was — and I had been living in South America. Now I had come to pick it up. My husband was dead and I had come back to Denmark to settle here again and make a new home based on all that we had shared in the past.

It was a summer's day. The rays of the afternoon sun still shone on the flowering roses, and everything was silent. Nobody moved in the garden and the roar of the busy city outside was nothing more than a faint accompaniment to the stillness. Deep in thought I sat down on a bench. Here I was with a hundred year-old picture book — cut, pasted up and 'edited' by a loving grandfather, and given to his granddaughter Christine on her third birthday. A writer of fairy tales, who was a friend of the family, had been sitting with grandfather cutting, pasting and dreaming up stories beside him with great charm and subtlety.

Little Christine took good care of her book, and it later formed part of the inheritance of her son — and only child — Knud Stampe Bardenfleth, and after him of her only grandchild, my husband Carl-Emil Bardenfleth. And now the book was mine. But was it really? What sort of life could it have with me, who had no children and so no one to whom it could be handed down? And yet it deserved life. First and foremost because of the spirit with which its makers imbued it, but also — more personally for me — because its three previous owners had all died in their prime. I wanted to make a memorial to them. The noise of the city had faded by the time I set out for home — pondering still, but without a clear answer to my question.

The answer now lies in front of you. I am deeply grateful to a good English friend of mine, Anthony le Maître, who first put forward the idea of printing the book and who made the first moves to carry out the plan, and to Mr Ole Woldbye who took on the task of supervising the photography of the plates with great devotion. I would also like to thank Dr Erik Dal for agreeing to provide the book with its commentary. He has drawn upon his wealth of knowledge in examining its many aspects and thus given further life and meaning to the whole.

Publication of the book marks the creation of a fund to be named *Christine Stampe's Picture Book*. All proceeds from the sale of the book in different countries will be placed in the fund, and its resources will later be used to support scholarly work in the humanities, especially in those areas which were of interest to the book's three previous owners: Danish history, the Danish language, Danish literature, and also music — including song. Eventually the original picture book will find a permanent place in the museum at Silkeborg, the Danish town whose growth owed so much to the paper mill owned by the Drewsen family. Finally, my warm thanks are due to those who have so readily agreed to administer the fund and unselfishly taken on the work that this involves.

Alette Bardenfleth

Alette Bardenfleth
Copenhagen
January 1984

INTRODUCTION

Hans Christian Andersen (1805-1875).
Photograph by Georg E. Hansen, 1862.

Christine's Picture Book is a scrapbook, and like all the best scrapbooks — and like diaries with the ink turned sepia, or bundles of dusty letters tied up with string — it is a modest document in the private history of a family. Although it was primarily the work of a man-of-affairs, Judge Drewsen (who stares a little haughtily across page 3 of this Introduction), and although he brought in as helper his old friend Hans Christian Andersen (who presides benignly at the head of this column), the work that they did was not intended to be any sort of public statement — neither artful narrative nor official record. It was a birthday-present for Drewsen's granddaughter Christine, and the focus of their attention was on the pleasure it would bring her as she turned the pages from one surprising scene to the next.

To get behind this document, to understand a little more about how its highly informal pages were assembled, it is perhaps worth considering the options and resources that were open to Messrs Drewsen and Andersen as compilers. (For large sections of the book may seem surprising to us as intended for a little girl just three years old).

In 1859, when the scraps were being brought together, Europe was already deep into the Great Age of Print. Ever since printing had been established as a workable process round about 1450, it had dominated European communications, but only after 1800 did its potential as a mass-medium come to be realised.

A series of new inventions, new techniques and new materials enabled presses to operate more rapidly and with more efficiency than ever before, and a reciprocal influence developed between the industry and a popular audience.

The increasing quantity and variety of goods turned out by the press stimulated a growth of interest in print, and this in turn encouraged manufacturers and publishers to try out further new ideas. From a concentration on simply made, and often rather dour-looking, books and periodicals, the industry began to expand and to exploit the possibilities of popular broadsheets, pamphlets and chap-books, newspapers, magazines and all manner of commercial printing. Techniques of illustration, and methods for reproducing illustration improved, and by the middle of the century there was a huge range of sources, apart from books, which were accessible to anyone interested in the compilation of scrapbooks.

It is true, and for our purpose significant, that much of this print was only of indirect interest to young children, so that one of the problems that Drewsen and Andersen may have faced was the selection of pictures which they could see as being attractive to Christine. Yet at the same time the mere collecting of scraps, in however haphazard a way, has a particular fascination, as can be observed in the formalizing of the activity in Ephemera Societies and the like. For while these trivia may not have the appeal of more expensive bits of paper like postage stamps, they offer wide scope to the imagination. Almost any piece of printing is grist to the scrapbook maker's mill, and most of it can be acquired without special expense. What matters is the eye of the selector and the wit or taste with which the material is managed.

From what Dr Erik Dal says in his Postscript to this book, and in his notes to the individual plates, we can perceive the background to Drewsen and

Andersen's editorial activities. They used the sort of sources that would be appreciated by any collector of printed ephemera today (even though such a one might have pained reservations about the chopping-up of individual printed units). Thus we can see on the very first page of the book examples of scraps from a commercial label and from a calendar, as well as a little picture that may have been cut from a *Bilderbogen* or picture-sheet. As we progress through the book's 123 plates we can imagine Adolph Drewsen collecting up suitable specimens from the variety of print that he came across day by day.

Here and there in the book are represented such items as a theatre advertisement (pl.1), a bookmark (pl.19), a menu (pl.105) and, in some-what greater quantity, fashion-plates, picture-cards and illustrations that may well have come from books. (It does not seem to have been Andersen or Drewsen's policy to dismember books for the sake of an illustration or two — but it may well be that pictures that came from children's books or travel books were the remnants of broken copies which were losing their plates anyway).

By far the greatest number of scraps in *Christine's Picture Book,* however, come from trade prospectuses and newspapers, from magazines — many of which were of German or French origin — and from that European phenomenon, the picture-sheet. The latter is not a form of popular printing that seems to have developed in Great Britain to the extent that it did in mainland Europe, where German and French examples were abundant. (It may well be that the more rapid penetration of the British market by print during the early nineteenth century — especially the wide distribution of chap-books, magazines and comic and political prints — curbed the development of the kind of picture-sheet production that flourished on the continent).

Certainly Britain enjoyed a huge output of toy-theatre materials which broadly belong in the picture-sheet category, and which are to be found on a number of pages of *Christine's Picture Book.* There was nothing in Britain, however, to correspond with the massive quantity of instruc-tive and entertaining sheets which Drewsen and

Andersen also used. Dr Dal traces in his notes the source of many of the pictures to *imageries* or *Bilderbogen,* and there are some occasions when whole sheets are used (e.g. pls 1, 10 and 109), but there can be little doubt that many of the untraced scraps also came from these sources — especially the little human and animal figures that are used to provide borders for, or to give balance to, many of the pages.

With regard to the expansion of the fashion for scrapbooks after 1859, it is worth noting that printers were stimulated to the production of picture-sheets solely for the use of scrap-paper collectors. Many of these were produced in Germany where there was huge production of gaudily printed, glazed and embossed sheets of flowers, animals and quaint people known as 'reliefs' or 'chromos'. These were widely imported into Britain in the last quarter of the nineteenth century by such firms as Birn Bros., Hildesheimer & Co., Marcus Ward, and many others.

Christine reading in front of her mother, Jonna Stampe.
Sepia drawing by P.C. Skovgaard, c. 1867.

As well as displaying something of the variety of popular printing of the 1850s, *Christine's Picture Book* also forms a small anthology of the reproduc-tive methods of the period. As we should expect, many of the pictures are reproduced by a standard process as old as printing itself: the simply cut wood-block, which gives an outline picture that can be printed alongside type. This basic mode of illustration can clearly be seen in the set of animal profiles on pl.38, where only the simplest effects of detail and shading are attempted, but where (as in many other instances) the result has been made less stark by the addition of hand-colouring.

Pictures like these could be cheaply and swiftly produced by cutting wood-blocks with a knife-blade on the lateral or plank grain. A far more sophisticated effect, however, might be obtained by engraving the much more responsive end-grain of the block with more refined tools. The craft of wood-engraving reached a high peak during the 1850s and 1860s and there are many examples of fine workmanship in *Christine's Picture Book*. The method can be seen, albeit in rigid, stylized form, in the English engraving on pl.39, but a measure of its potential, in conjunction with hand-colouring appears in the elaborate page-borders etc. shown on pl.7 and in many other instances throughout the book.

While woodcuts and wood-engravings are the predominant means for reproducing pictures in these scraps, there is a sufficient body of examples to testify to the growing use of lithography. This method, which allows pictures to be printed from a flat rather than a raised or incised surface, is very hospitable to freely drawn lines and to conveying gradations of tone (something of these qualities can be seen in the monochrome lithographs placed above the wood-engraving on pl.39). There are a fair number of lithographed drawings throughout the picture book, and when hand-coloured these can have much warmth and subtlety (e.g. pl.5). At the same time, though, in a few instances, the emergence of chromo-lithography can be seen, where the image — colours and all — is entirely produced from the lithographic stones (e.g. pl.16). In these cases, Christine is being offered some of the earliest successes of industrialized colour printing.

Apart from these reproductive methods, of which there are many examples, one could also note a few occasions when the chilly but highly detailed craft of steel engraving is to be found (e.g. pl.12). Here the design is cut, and possibly etched as well, into the surface of the metal plate, and its reproduction is achieved by covering the surface with ink, and then wiping it clean again, so that only the ink-filled incisions will print. And in

addition to that standard but fairly costly method of reproduction, the book also includes two examples of the nineteenth century's eager experi-mentation in graphic processes: the chemitype on pl.79 and the chalkotype on pl.121.

Of more consequence than analysing the sources which Drewsen and Andersen used and the graphic styles of the period, however, is the

Adolph Drewsen (1803-1885). Portrait in oils by Wilhelm Marstrand, 1850.

way that the authors set about selecting from their hoard of pictures and organizing the individual pages of the book. For it is at this point that Christine and the Stampe family and the Drewsen family come to the fore, while we moderns turn into intrusive spectators. As Dr Dal suggests in his Postscript, Adolph Drewsen and Hans Christian Andersen may have been making their scrapbook for the fun of it, but they were also doing it with a close awareness of its immediate audience. Many common interests, topics of the moment, or family jokes would be in the forefront of their minds as they worked at their cutting and pasting, and many of what seem to us to be the oddities of the book may well have made particular sense to those who first looked at it. Pages may also have been compiled with an eye to the talk that could arise as Christine turned to them.

Even so, it is not always easy to fathom how certain choices were made or how certain combinations of pictures have come into being. Very often the scrapbook seems no more than a tumultuous medley of visual impressions which harmonize with variable success (as Dr Dal points out, it seems almost perverse that the linked sequence of 'Stations of the Cross' pictures on pls 34 and 107 should not only be separated but should also appear back to front).

On the other hand, there is, throughout the book, a continuing sense of the comic possibilities of unusual juxtapositions, which is supplemented by the inclusion of a variety of (often adult) caricatures and jokes; and there is a scrapbook maker's proper feeling for the balance and arrangement of pictures on the page, a point reinforced rather than contradicted by the hectic collages on pls 68 and 99.

The other unifying factor in the book is the personal involvement of its authors, most famously demonstrated in the presence of five examples of Andersen's skill as a maker of paper-cuts which are widely acknowledged as being among his best, and which display the diverse effects that he was able to achieve.

Along with these individual contributions go the little doggerel verses that the two men — often perhaps on impulse — scribbled among the pictures. Here the personal quality of *Christine's Picture Book* is most obvious, not just because of the personal references that can be found in the verses: 'Og dette skal være Christines Skaal!' (pl.17) or 'Her har Viggo og Andersen kjørt' (pl.20), but because of the relaxed familiarity of friends enjoying a private joke.

Undoubtedly, so far as the preparation of an English edition of this volume is concerned, the informal, not to say amateurish character of these verses poses insoluble problems. Their offhand, colloquial, and sometimes punning style would have made any literal prose translation sound ridiculous, and yet to make a verse translation is to run the risk of appearing to force the humour, or to be naively simple, where in fact the original

demands just such a response. In the event, this second method was ineluctable, and I have tried hard throughout to match both the verbal patterns and the sense of these tiny verses. On a number of occasions I have been defeated, either by the brevity of the text or the intractability of the rhyme scheme, and there I have not hesitated to interpret the verse more loosely or to invent something which looked like an English equivalent. Since in all cases a transcription of the original has been printed, Danish scholars will be able to see the extent of the changes.

In all these instances, however, the most important thing, both in the translation and in the making of the facsimile itself, is the spontaneity and intimacy of *Christine's Picture Book*. Those involved in the often complex process of making a late-twentieth century printed book have tried not to lose sight of the fact that it originated in the birthday celebrations for a little girl and that it is thereby a memento of the warmth that could subsist in nineteenth century family life.

Brian Alderson
Richmond, North Yorkshire
January 1984

Christine: Hvisses er denne Billedbog?
Morfaer: Kanske Christines?
Christine; glad, forlegen, men tier.
Morfaer: DER har Du den!

Christine: Whose's picture book's this?
Grandfather: What if it's Christine's?
Christine looks pleased, shy, says nothing.
Grandfather: THERE you are!

This title-page, like many another, was made when the rest of the book was complete and then pasted in. 'Kjøbenhavn' comes from a lithographed label, another part of which can be found on pl. 59. The heavy, shaded letters, typical of the advertising of the period, come from the displayed word 'KALENDER' for 1859 (the picture book made for Christine's sister Rigmor has the word ENDE cut out in similar letters).

Andersen himself refers to this kind of treatment of title-pages in his story 'Godfather's Picture Book' (1868): 'Look; that's the first page of the book; that's like a playbill'. The introduction to Astrid Stampe's picture book also includes a little dialogue between grandfather and child with the sort of childish turn of phrase we find above in Christine's question, rendered in translation 'Whose's picture book's this?'

Christine: Hvisfor er denne Billedbog?

Morfaer: Lauken Christines?

Christine; glad, forlegen, men dine.

Morfaer:  har du den!

DER

KJÖBENHAVN

den 30te October

1859

PLATE 1

A programme from the Copenhagen variety hall, the Alhambra. It is certainly the oldest such item to survive, and is as mixed in its content as *Christine's Picture Book*. It is set in a style of type known as 'Fraktur' which was still widely used in Denmark at this time, and even more so in Germany. The small pictures are all pasted on except for the two printed on either side of the heading.

The Alhambra staged popular indoor concerts, open air shows, pantomimes by itinerant per-formers, and evenings of dance music and illu-minations. The theatre was planned by Georg Carstensen (1812-57) but did not open until after his death. The enterprising Carstensen, whom Andersen much admired, created Copenhagen's famous Tivoli in 1843, and a mixed winter-garden Casino (later a theatre, see pls 52 and 111) in 1847. The Alhambra finally opened to compete with the Tivoli which was being run by Carstensen's succes-sor (see pls 56 and 63).

ALHAMBRA.

Nr. 57.   **4 Sk.**

Fredagen den 9. Juli 1858.

Festens Begyndelse tilkjendegives ved Kanonsalut

og

Kl. 5: „Festmarsch" af et stort Musikcorps fra Alhambra's Taarne.

J Concertsalen:

Stor Concert i 4 Afdelinger, fra Kl. $6\frac{1}{2}$—$11\frac{1}{2}$, under Anførsel af Hr. Musikdirecteur A. F. Lincke.

Første Afdeling Kl. $6\frac{1}{2}$.

1. Horneman: Dannebrogsmarsch.
2. Kuhlau: Ouverture til „Elverhøi".
3. Lincke: Emily=Vals.
4. Fröhlich: Finale af „Waldemar".
5. Lumbye: En Sommernat paa Møens Klint, Galop.

Anden Afdeling Kl. $7\frac{3}{4}$.

6. Gade: Ouverture til „Mariotta".
7. Strauss: Volkssänger, Vals.
8. Ahlström: Nordisk Folkemusik.
9. Lumbye: Champagne=Galop.

Tredie Afdeling Kl. 9.

10. Gade: Imellem Fjeldene, Ouverture.
11. Horneman: Alhambra=Tappenstreg.
12. Svensk, norsk og dansk Nationalsang.
13. Lincke: Congres=Galop (ny).

Fjerde Afdeling Kl. 10.

14. Fröhlich: Introduction til „Waldemar".
15. Lanner: Hoffnungs=Strahlen, Vals.
16. Lincke: Fantasi over danske Sange.
17. Horneman: Frederik den des Tappenstreg.
18. Lumbye: En Tour paa Dyrehavsbakken, Galop.

Paa Theatret i Haven:

Jmellem Concertens 1ste og 2den og 2den og 3die Afdeling:

Magiske Forestillinger, af Magikeren Hr. A. v. Olivo, hvoriblandt:

„Kunsten at gaae til Alhambra og blive gratis beværtet",

samt flere nye Kunststykker.

Kl. $9\frac{3}{4}$ Djævlemøllen eller Pjerrot som Barnepige,

Comisk Pantomime i 1 Act.

Personerne:

Cassander.   Columbine, hans Datter.   Harlequin, gift med Columbine.   Pjerrot, deres Barnepige.   Sybille, en gammel Her. 2 Djævle.

Paa Plainen:

Kl. $6\frac{1}{2}$ Brydning med Stokke, Udstødning af Ringen, Klattring, Vippespring og „Hvem napper Støvlerne",

Comiske Lege, udføres af Drenge.

Kl. 5-1 Horumusik.

Kl. 10-1 Dandse=Musik fra Tribunen.

Hele Hovedbygningen bliver festlig smykket og decoreret.

J Chiosken tilvenstre er anbragt

en smuk decoreret Vaabenhalle.

Kl. 9-1 Stort Bauxhall

af **6000 Lamper** og

Hovedbygningen brillant illumineret ind= og udvendig.

J Nærheden af Dandsepladsen er anlagt en

Bacchus-Kilde.

PLATE 2

Shakespeare has it that all the world's a stage, but the stage can also be a world, as this French picture shows, a 'cosmos' dispensing 'gratis' both 'quality' and 'esprit'. The orchestral players belong to the original picture, while the six actors on the stage and the small figures at top and bottom are pasted on, enlivening as well as partly obscuring the main picture.

It is entirely in keeping with Andersen's feeling for the theatre that this book begins with the programme of an entertainment and a scene in a theatre. As a boy he sang in the chorus at the opera and studied at the Royal Theatre ballet school, and the stage continued to fascinate him all his life. He must have attended thousands of performances, yet was never successful as a playwright.

PLATE 3

Mikkel kan ikke la' Gjassene gaae.
Lotte og Erik saae derpaa.

Lotte and Erik watch the geese
That Reynard will not leave in peace.

The upper pictures have a rather old-fashioned look. *Lotte* and *Erik* were common names, but if they here allude to particular children, it is not to members of the Stampe or Drewsen families. 'Lotte' probably comes from a caption using the word 'Lotteri'.

Lotte

Mikkel Fan idu la' Gjæsim gaae.
Latte og Erik sana Dreya. —

ERIK

PLATE 4

Jorden er hvid – den ligger med Snee,
Prosessionen er sort, det kan hver Mand see!
Aligevel ere de Alle glade!
Prinds Tusindskjøn skal paa Maskerade!

White is the garden under the snow
Black the procession — see how they go!
Everyone's happy in that parade:
The Prince of a Thousand Beauties is off
to the masquerade!

Prindsesse Tusindskjøn, Princess of a Thousand Beauties (not *Prince),* was a book or fairy tale with silhouettes by the master-silhouettist Karl Fröhlich (1821-98). This reproduction comes from a German publisher's advertisement (Stuttgart 1857). The technique would have interested Andersen, himself a maker of silhouettes. To the left is a bust of Goethe and to the right the word NI which means 'nine' in Danish. It is not clear where the letters come from or what they signify.

The cartoons below are also German. The left hand one may be translated as follows: 'A waggish fellow was at a dinner party with thirteen at table. When someone remarked on this with some consternation, he replied, "Never mind, I'll eat enough for two."' The cartoon on the right portrays a farmer and a yokel in a field. 'Farmer: Aren't you ashamed of yourself lying there sleeping? You're not fit for anything under the sun. Yokel: That's why I'm lying in the shade.'

Prinzeß Tausendschön.

[illegible]
[illegible]
[illegible]
Prinzeß Tausendschön [illegible] zur Maskerade!

Als ein Witzbold in einer Gesellschaft war, in welcher dreizehn Personen am Tische saßen, und dies Einer mit Schrecken bemerkte, sagte jener: „Beruhigen Sie sich, ich esse für Zwei."

Bauer. Schämst Du Dich nicht, Dich hier hin zu legen und zu schlafen? Du bist ja nicht werth, daß Dich die Sonne bescheint.

Knecht. Deßwegen habe ich mich auch hier in den Schatten gelegt.

PLATE 5

Halen
Gjør mere Lykke end Talen!

Der Pfau,
Det er nok Tysk. au!

His tail so long
Is prettier than his song.

'Der Pfau'
That must be German — ow!

These two birds come from a fine German series, which is also used elsewhere. A whole sheet — possibly a plate from a serious book — has been used here, though it can scarcely have been intended for cutting up. All the small figures have been added.

Hahn
Hört man Ryder und Dulder!

Der Pfau,
Ist ur noch hyß au!

Argus

PLATE 6

The combination of black letter and Roman type (respectively German and French) in the captions to these pictures closely resembles the lettering on a sheet issued by F.G. Schulz in Stuttgart (see illus. 173 in Wolfgang Brückner's *Populäre Druckgraphik Europas: Deutschland,* Munich, 1969). The subjects, which come from around the Mediterranean, are: a half natural, half artificial rocky gateway in Algeria; Achmed Pasha, the Bey of Tunis (presumably Sidi Achmed, who visited Paris in 1846 and then sought to Europeanize his court); pilgrims resting on the way from Mecca; a Kazbah and a caravan ('Kazbah' signifies the highest and possibly fortified quarter of a town, here perhaps in Algeria); the Acropolis at Athens; an innkeeper from Andalusia; the island of Marguerite, presumably at Monaco; an Egyptian tomb and sailing ships; a Moorish boy on an ass; and lastly, a bold and successful quest for herrings.

Andersen was constantly attracted to the south — and not just to Italy. In 1841 he visited the Balkans and Asia Minor, and in the 1860s he went to Spain, Portugal and Algeria.

Dies Felsenthor auf Algiers Flur
Schuf halb die Kunst halb die Natur.
La poste en Alger à la plus grande part
Fut faite par la nature et non pas par l'art.

Was dieser Posador wohl treibt?
Ich denke wohl er trinkt u. schreibt.
Un Posador Andalousien
Qui boit et écrit très bien.

Der Bey von Tunis blickt gar wild
Hier sehet ihr sein stolzes Bild.
C'est Achmed Pacha, Bey de Tunis
Dont le fierté jamais ne finit.

Die Insel Marguerite hat
Ganz dicht am Ufer eine Stadt.
L'île de Sainte Marguerite pacifique
A sur son bord une ville magnifique.

Die Pilger Mecca's ruhn an diesem Ort,
Und setzen dann gestärkt die Reise fort.
Les pélerins se reposent à ce lieu
Etant soulagés ils dirent à la Mecque adieu.

Beim Grabmahl in Egyptens Land
Sieht man hier Schiffe an dem Strand.
On peut voir en Egypte cette tombe belle
Beaucoup des vaisseaux passent auprès d'elle.

Am Kasbah-Platz der Leute Schaar
Weilt mit Kameel u. Dromedar.
A la place de Kasbah, bien des gens
Avec leurs chameaux se sont reposants.

Ein Maurenknabe reitet hier
Dahin auf seinem Eselthier.
Un garçon Moor, qui maintenant
Va sur un âne patient.

Hier auf dem Berge sehet ihr stehn
Die alte Akropolis von Athen.

Wenn man sich regt so braucht man nicht lang
Zu einem reichlichen Haringsfang.

PLATE 7

(see previous page)

Of the two rectangular designs, the right hand one is presumably the title-page of a German annual on which the age-old tradition of personifying the seasons of the year is linked to images which signify childhood, youth, maturity and old age. The title and year have been cut away. The left hand design comes from the prospectus for a work on Central Africa, but the six heads that have been superimposed are not by any means all African. On the small woman's head at the bottom, see pl.43.

PLATE 8

A further scene in which the round design is probably related to the seasons (note the year date below). On the back of the picture is a German text whose central section is about Princess Augusta of Prussia (cf. pl. 93). The mixture of scenes in the upper right-hand picture is integral to the print; it is not a group put together by the authors.

PLATE 9

Her staaer en Hyrde saa ung og fiin.
Han blæser i Guld og høres af Sviin.
H. C. Andersen

Her staaer den gamle Nicolai,
Han har hverken Trøie, eiheller Cavai,
Men Skjorteærmer og en Vest af Bai.

Hvor skinner med Guld hendes røde Trøie,
Den skinner dog ikke, som hendes Øie.

Look at this pig-man, so young and fine,
He blows a gold trumpet and looks after the swine.
H.C. Andersen

Look at old Nicolas going his ways
Without jacket or jumper on working days —
He's down to his shirt sleeves and waistcoat of baize.

There's a glint of gold in her jumper's seams
But it doesn't gleam as her eye gleams.

The first of several pages with pretty hand-coloured French lithographs about country life. (See also pls 19, 31, 96 and 104). The two additions are a relief print of golden corn and a bit of paper with the English word 'flax' near the distaff which the shepherdess carries.

Le berger du village.

Hu... ...an... ...
...
...
...
J. ... ...

Nicolai.   *Les Chasseurs.*   *La bergère et ses moutons.*

Jean le laboureur.   *hue donc Fanfan*

PLATE 10

A sheet showing the French headquarters in the Crimean War and sharpshooters at the siege of Sebastopol, which ended with the fall of the city on 9 September 1855. This is one of the few extended examples in the book of a genre that was very popular with boys and men: picture sheets of soldiers which could be pasted on to card and then cut out. It was printed during, or at least prompted by, the Crimean War (1853–6) which preoccupied Europe at the time and proved to be a major political event, as well as a subject for entertainment and satire.

The sheet is signed 'Glémarec'. This printer, who moved to Paris from the provinces, was one of the last to use woodcuts in sheets of this kind, even though he was also a lithographer. Most of Glémarec's work dates from 1845 to 1860, but some of his wood-blocks were from older stock. The soldiers seem to have been coloured by stencil, although hand-colouring was thought to give a better finish. Various contemporary accounts exist of picture sheets being coloured in workshops and even at home by families. The work was paid for at piece-work rates. (See also pl. 109).

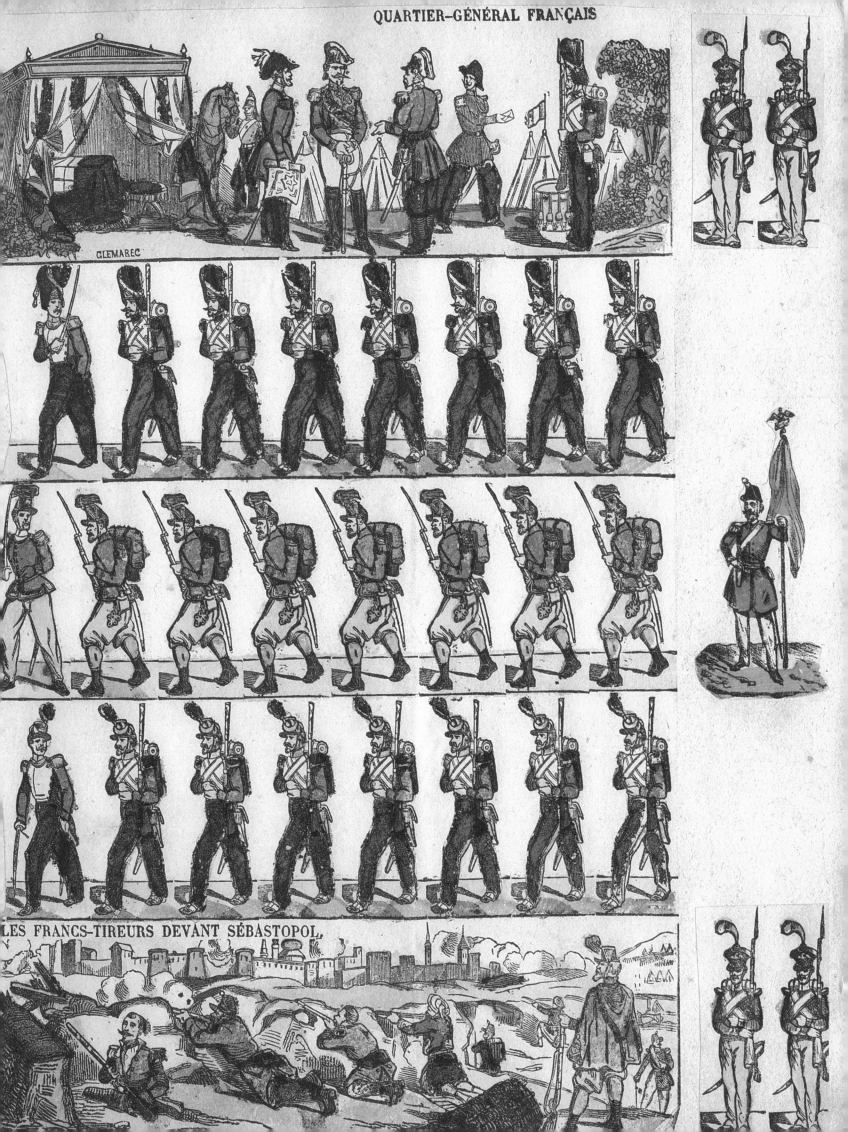

QUARTIER-GÉNÉRAL FRANÇAIS

GLEMAREC

LES FRANCS-TIREURS DEVANT SÉBASTOPOL.

———————————— PLATE 11 ————————————

Christine's Picture Book contains only five of Andersen's paper-cuts, but some of these are among his finest work in the genre (see pls 18, 59, 80 and 91). This symmetrical design is rather disfigured by the poultry round its edges, but is otherwise very characteristic. The central wheel is more finely cut than that on pl. 18, but not as fine as another in which the spokes are made to take on human form. Swans are a permanent element in Andersen's imagination and in his paper-cuts and, along with mermaids, are among the few motifs common to both his stories and his silhouettes. Between the palm trees at the top and bottom of the design are two of the many troll heads that appear in Andersen's paper-cuts.

PLATE 19

'The Grape Harvest' (centre) is from the French series mentioned in the note to pl. 9. It is flanked by the religious designs 'Penitence' and 'The Gift of Wisdom'. These were probably intended as book-marks for devotional works; they have been cut out by hand and not stamped out like later glazed pictures. Similar designs are found in one of the modest works made for Rigmor Stampe by Adolph Drewsen on his own (now in the possession of Mrs Estrid Faurholt of Copenhagen).

There are counterparts of 'The Academician' and 'The Nursemaid' (animals dressed up in clothes) on pls 105 and 110, with or without their captions. The label, which has had its central name or note of contents cut away to make room for a little country scene, is Danish and was printed by J.L. Sivertsen who ran a book and lithographic printshop in the centre of Copenhagen from 1849 to 1863 (see pl. 96).

LA PÉNITENCE

Les vendanges.

DON DE SAGESSE

Académicien

Bonne de enfant

PLATE 20

Her har Viggo og Andersen kjø(rt)
Derom har lille Christine hør(t).

Little Christine has heard us say
That Viggo and Andersen drove this way.

'Reise', which means 'journey' in both Danish and German, is the theme of a page which takes the reader through a series of such dramatic scenes as 'the Niagara Falls in North America' and 'the way out from the Via Mala' (a wild chasm in southern Switzerland where two tributaries of the Rhine meet between the Splügen and Bernardin mountains). Despite much investigation, the 'Three Devil's Arrows' has not been traced, and may be a Romantic or pre-Romantic artifact designed to look like a real ancient monument. All the prints are from German periodicals: 'Niagara' has an advertisement for the *Illustriertes Prämien-Journal* of 1857-8 on its reverse side (cf. pl. 49). For the centre picture see pl. 61.

'Viggo' was Christine's uncle, Viggo Drewsen, who as a young man in 1852 accompanied Andersen on a journey through Germany and Switzerland. They went over the Via Mala on 1 July on the way from Chur to Chiavenna and, according to Andersen's diary, it was 'magnificent and sobering, but with rain — all the time rain.' Andersen saw the place again on 2 July 1873 and wrote 'From the second bridge in the Via Mala the Rhine was so far down and so hemmed in with cliffs that it seemed to be just a tunnel.' (*Dagbøger* III and X, Copenhagen, 1974-5).

Die drei Teufelspfeile.

Ausgang der Via Mala.

Der Niagara-Fall in Nord-Amerika.

PLATE 21

The top picture is a large wood engraving, reminiscent of many Cairo street scenes, by Karl Girardet in the *Magasin Pittoresque* (1855). Egypt, ancient and modern, was an extremely popular subject at the time. The bottom picture, from *Die illustrirte Welt* (1858, p. 240), illustrates an anonymous romance set in France, *Das wilde Thier* ('The Wild Beast'), which ran for over twenty-one issues. There are German literary texts on the back of both engravings.

The figure at the bottom right is a 'nisse' or brownie, a small supernatural being who was at this date establishing himself as a Danish character: a friendly old man with a beard and a red cap, who would later be associated with Christmas. He has here been cut out of a newspaper advertisement for the humorous periodical *Folkets Nisse*. The 'nisse' also figures in Andersen's story 'The Brownie at the Grocer's', and before that in 'The Travelling Companion'.

—————— PLATE 22 ——————

Rød i Kammen,
Rød i Hammen.

Jeg troer, at Svanen
Er utilpas hos Pelicanen.

Red comb
Red colour.

It looks to me as though the swan
Is ill at ease with the pelican.

This is the first use made in the book of a fine series of French bird prints, hand-coloured lithographs, also to be seen on pls 25, 37, 74, 118, and elsewhere without captions.

4. Le Paon.

Le Bouvreuil.

Le Tigé.

Le Pélican.　　　25. Le Cygne.

PLATE 23

Hun har Ædderkop Figur
Fik og Ædderkop Natur.

I Munden en Sut
Faaer den søde Snut.

Waspish features
Waspish nature.

Baby's dummy
With love from mummy.

An effective juxtaposition of two large wood engravings from a German periodical. It is not inconceivable that both illustrate the same story.

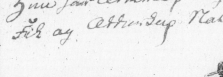

PLATE 24

Der løber en Tyv, han er gruelig bange,
Han veed, han er ved at tages til Fange!

Han var som Slikmund reent af lave,
Nu gaaer han med en daarlig Mave!

What fear the running robber feels
The dog will lay him by the heels!

Too many sweets and too much cake
Have given him the tummy-ache!

Der løber en Tyr! han er grulig bange,
han med, han er alt at løbe til fange!

Han var som Slikvand vant af lam.
Nu gaar han med en dvarlig Masa!

PLATE 25

Another fine selection of French bird prints. At the bottom left is a giant auk (*gejrfugl* in Danish). Similar in size to a wild goose, this creature was unable to fly, and indeed could hardly walk. It became extinct through man's exploitation around 1840. There are pictures of it in catalogues from the private museum of the doctor and archaeologist Ole Worm (Copenhagen 1655). The swan, as has been mentioned elsewhere in the book, was one of Andersen's favourite birds.

7. *La Brève des Philippines.*   8. *La Mainate.*   9. *Le Jaseur.*   10.

—— PLATE 26 ——

Hønen paa sit Værksted,
hun lægger Æg.

Hønen opdrager sine Smaa.

Den smukkeste er jeg!
jeg er sort.

Hønen ruger ud, endnu ere
de grønne.

Den deiligste er jeg, for
jeg er hvid!

Den stolteste.

Naboerne ere i Strid.

The hen has gone into her workshop,
She's laid an egg.

The hen brings up her brood.

I'm the smartest!
I'm black.

The eggs hatch out, and now —
green chickens!

I'm the prettiest because
I'm white!

The proudest.

Quarrelling neighbours.

This collection of scenes from a hen run calls to mind 'The Ugly Duckling' and 'In the Duck Yard'. A pun is intended in the fourth caption, where the chickens have been caught up in the colouring of the grass; the Danish 'grønne' (green) can imply extreme youth, as in English.

Hönan gaar til Nordpol,
hun lägger Æg!

Hönan opdrager sin Ţ...

Den smukkeste er jeg!
jeg er stolt!

Den dueligste er jeg, for
jeg er fri!!

Hönan väger ud, andan w
de grenen

Den Stolte!

PLATE 27

Pretty, colourful butterflies, more or less well reproduced, are to be found in the picture-sheets of many publishers. There are similar, though not identical, illustrations throughout *Christine's Picture Book*.

Two stories by Andersen, 'The Dung Beetle' and 'The Butterfly', date from this period; the latter has to do with a butterfly wooing flowers, though without much success.

PLATE 28

Her seer Du Naturen tam og mild,
Der mede kneiser den ganske vild!

Here see nature meek and mild,
But underneath she's getting wild.

These two exotic wood engravings were cut in Leipzig by W. Georgy (1819-87), an illustrator much sought after at the time for his treatment of natural history subjects. On the back of the pictures is an advertisement for a botanical work. The vine stems twining across the top of the page are from a German source (see also pl. 12).

Hier harrt die Natürwelt dein, o mild
Wird wächst die deutsche Landschaft wild!

PLATE 29

Den Ene her har Intet paa,
Den Anden kan i Guld-Stads gaae,
Dog Sviin er disse begge to,
Og deres Moder var en So!

Først de Store, saa de Smaa,
Efter Rangen skal det gaae!

Here is one who's got no clothes on,
And one who's got a golden coat on,
Here's a pig, and here's another,
And both have got a sow for a mother.

First the larger, then the smaller
Lined up in a proper order.

PLATE 30

The toucan, the parrot and the ostrich are picture   Three small pictures have been grouped round it.
prints; the emu is an illustration from a book.

LORIOT.   **GIRAFE.**   **KAKATOÈS.** *La Loutre*

Pas peur du feu.

CHAMEAU.   **DINDON.**   **HIPPOPOTAME.**

Didon dina, dit on, du dos d'un dodu dindon.

HÉRON.   **JOCKO.**   **FAISAN.**

WACCA   PANTHÈRE   QUINCAJOU

PLATE 39

The upper lithographs make up a plate from a German reference work whose title has not been established. They show early Indian, Greek and Egyptian concepts of the world, with a picture of the Greek chariot of the sun (rather curiously flanked on either side by an English lion and unicorn). Indian motifs from the same source were used by Drewsen in one of Rigmor Stampe's minor picture books (cf. pl. 19).

C.F. Sargent's engraving of the temple at Madura, the capital of Madras, with its 999 columns, is almost certainly unique in the book in coming from an English magazine, though Drewsen used a little more English material in other books. Sargent specialized in drawing landscapes for reproduction as wood engravings.

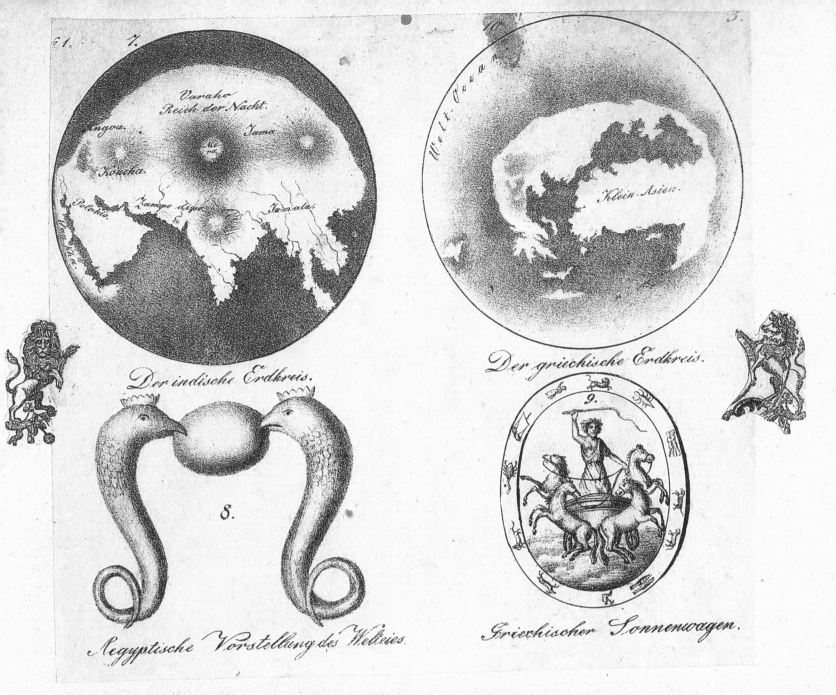

Der indische Erdkreis.

Der griechische Erdkreis.

8.

9.

Aegyptische Vorstellung des Weltkreis.

Griechischer Sonnenwagen.

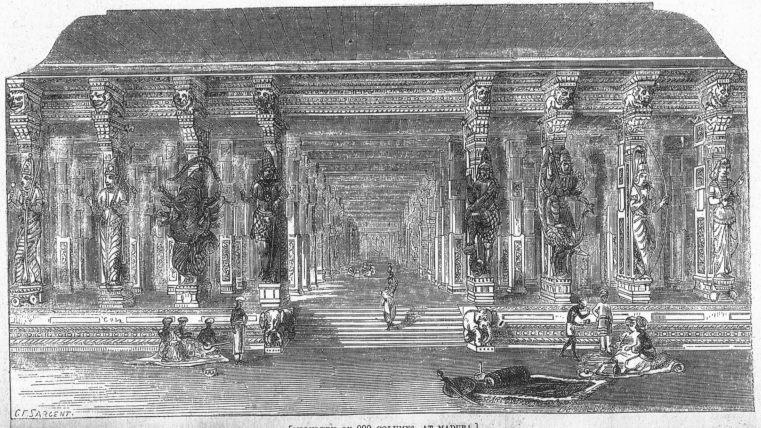

[CHOULTRY OF 999 COLUMNS, AT MADURA.]

PLATE 40

See til at skruppe a,
Prindsessen vil jeg ha!

Clear off, thee!
The princess is for me!

'The Wounded Knight' and 'Euricie Freed by Sir Alceste' belong to the series mentioned on pl. 17. An apt addition is the printed Danish rhyme from a cracker pasted below the top picture ('Behold within her eye/A blue and cloudless sky'). The scene in the centre also draws upon the tradition of medieval chivalry.

Of the small additions, the two at the bottom are the coat of arms of Denmark and Copenhagen, while the arms above right appear in frequent advertisements in the newspapers for the 'Gold-berger Rheumatic Chain' — a bimetallic chain with a galvanic current, which was worn as a remedy for rheumatism. The wreath used in pl. 49 also comes from a Goldberger advertisement. A competing apparatus, 'J. Hoffmann's portable hydro-electric rheumatic chains made after the English original', went so far as to put the English coat of arms on its advertisements (see also pl. 50).

Chevalier blessé.

En Himmel mild og klar
Er i Dit Øiepar.

Euricie délivrée par le Chevalier Alceste.

—— PLATE 41 ——

Telegraph Efterretning.
Paa Søndag opføres i China
Øehlenslægers Tragedie: Dina

Telegraphic intelligence.
On Sunday they perform in China
Oehlenschläger's tragedy *Dinah.*

'In China, you know, the Emperor's Chinese, and everybody round him is Chinese too'. Andersen's story 'The Nightingale', whose opening words are known the world over, offers broad perspectives on both art and life, but is also a reflection of the contemporary taste for chinoiserie shown in picture-sheets like this (see also pls 45 and 55). The long German article pasted below — possibly based on an English piece — is about the Chinese practice of fattening horses for food, until they weigh as much as 1000lb. The article begins in a chatty way, but it later makes use of first-hand 'technical' reports. On the back are articles about travelling in Lapland and slave-ownership among ants which suggest that the article comes from one of the popular periodicals of the day, in which travel and far away countries were favourite subjects.

Like much else in China, this strange method of horse-breeding has a long history. The article has therefore been decorated with a Danish subtitle which reads 'Old but good'. And Andersen has added another joke in his manuscript reference to the historical, but by no means Chinese, tragedy *Dinah* by the great Danish writer Oehlenschläger, who died in 1850. Furthermore, admiration for his dead friend H.C. Ørsted, and for all technical progress, prompts Andersen to foresee telegraphic communication with China!

Die chinesischen Mastpferde.

…ist ein sonderbares Land, das …e Reich der Mitte. Je mehr wir …lbe kennen lernen, desto mehr fin-… wir, daß man dort fast Alles hat … meist schon längst gehabt hat, …man bei uns findet. So erfah-… wir aus einem französischen Reise-… …e, daß in China die Jagd nach …graphen eben so herrscht, wie bei … nur daß sie dort weit älter ist. …eine geschriebene Zeile einer Per-… …des Alterthums wird ein fabelhaf-… …Preis bezahlt, und in Peking ist …in eigener Zweig der Industrie, …e Autographen zu verfertigen, …wie bei uns, wo man z. B. un-… …t einen Fabrikanten von Schiller-… …graphen entdeckte. Gewisse Ver-… …rungen des modernen europäi-… …Lebens kannten die Chinesen schon …e vor uns. Stumme Instrumente für Uebende, damit …urch ihre Töne nicht die Ohren zerreißen, Schießpulver …einimpfung, Buchdruckerei, Journale, Gesetzbücher, Klubbs, …reime, Anwendung des thierischen Magnetismus, Kennt-… …des irdischen, Droschken sind bei ihnen sehr alt. Sie …n Pfandleihhäuser unter Ueberwachung der Regierung, …die Neujahrsbesuche sind bei ihnen ein uralter Brauch. …noch nicht zu lange ist man bei uns auf den Einfall …mmen, anstatt seinen Glückwunsch selbst zu überbringen, …Karte abzugeben — die Chinesen senden einander seit …Jahren am Neujahrstage Glückwünschungskarten. …elegante Welt in China hält Pferde und Wagen, und …hört zum feinen Ton, selbst zu fahren; es giebt dort …kutschen und Fiaker. In den Schauspielhäusern sind …rre und mehrere Reihen Logen. Selbst Klubbs für …arische Unterhaltung sind seit undenklichen Zeiten in …rauch. C'est tout comme chez nous!

…Auch Handelsgärtner sind in China. Gardeners chro-… …erzählt uns von dem Besuch des Herrn R. Fortune …einem Handelsgarten zu Schangaë in China. Die …t Schangaë zählt ungeachtet ihres beträchtlichen Han-… …dennoch nur wenige reiche Einwohner. Man sieht …nicht die schönen Gärten der Mandarinen, welche man …ngpo bewundert; dagegen bieten die dortigen Handels-… …n viel Interesse. Ungefähr 2 engl. Meilen von der …t liegt einer der beträchtlichsten derselben, welcher unter …Namen „Garten des Südens" bekannt ist. Aus diesem …en erhielt Herr Fortune eine Menge von Pflanzen, welche …ach seiner ersten Reise in China in England einführte. …In einem großen einstöckigen Hause wohnt die ganze …ilie des Gärtners, eines alten Mannes, nebst zwei ver-

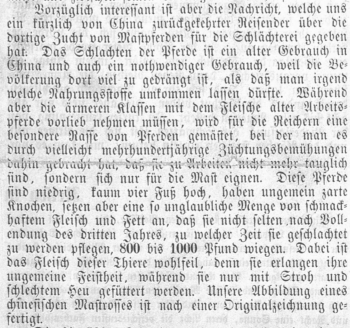

Gammelt men godt.

heiratheten Söhnen und Töchtern und vielen Enkeln. Es ist überhaupt Sitte der Chinesen, daß Eltern, Kinder und Kindeskinder in einem großen Stamm- hause beisammen wohnen, und nur selten kommt es vor, daß irgend ein Glied der Familie dasselbe verläßt, um sich anderswo anzusiedeln.

Sehr freundlich wurde Herr For- tune von dem alten Gärtner und dessen Sohn empfangen, und eifrig erkundigten sie sich nach den bei der ersten Reise mitgenommenen Pflanzen: ob dieselben gut in England angekom- men wären und ob sie dort Aufsehen gemacht hätten. Nicht wenig erfreut waren sie, als sie erfuhren, welches Aufsehen manche in ihrem Garten er- worbene Pflanzen erregt hätten. — In der Mitte des Gartens erhebt sich ein mit Blumen bekränzter Hügel, unter welchem die Vor- fahren des alten Gärtners ruhen, so wie auch er dereinst dort unter und zwischen seinen Lieblingen die Ruhe finden wird.

Vorzüglich interessant ist aber die Nachricht, welche uns ein kürzlich von China zurückgekehrter Reisender über die dortige Zucht von Mastpferden für die Schlächterei gegeben hat. Das Schlachten der Pferde ist ein alter Gebrauch in China und auch ein nothwendiger Gebrauch, weil die Be- völkerung dort viel zu gedrängt ist, als daß man irgend welche Nahrungsstoffe umkommen lassen dürfte. Während aber die ärmeren Klassen mit dem Fleische alter Arbeits- pferde vorlieb nehmen müssen, wird für die Reichern eine besondere Rasse von Pferden gemästet, bei der man es durch vielleicht mehrhundertjährige Züchtungsbemühungen dahin gebracht hat, daß sie zu Arbeiten nicht mehr tauglich sind, sondern sich nur für die Mast eignen. Diese Pferde sind niedrig, kaum vier Fuß hoch, haben ungemein zarte Knochen, setzen aber eine so unglaubliche Menge von schmack- haftem Fleisch und Fett an, daß sie nicht selten, nach Voll- endung des dritten Jahres, zu welcher Zeit sie geschlachtet zu werden pflegen, 800 bis 1000 Pfund wiegen. Dabei ist das Fleisch dieser Thiere wohlfeil, denn sie erlangen ihre ungemeine Feistheit, während sie nur mit Stroh und schlechtem Heu gefüttert werden. Unsere Abbildung eines chinesischen Mastrosses ist nach einer Originalzeichnung ge- fertigt.

Die chinesischen Schweine, welche ebenfalls bei geringer Mast ein ungemeines Gewicht erlangen, sind bereits allge- mein bekannt; vielleicht werden nächstens auch chinesische Mastpferde bei uns eingeführt werden.

PLATE 42

En Gaasegang skulde Du have,
To Gjæs dog kom aflave.

All these geese should walk in line,
But two of them are not inclined.

En Gaasegang skilte du Jann,
to Gjæs dog bare aflann. —

de Hunde lage Hyot forsecht,
der brave Hand den Guide fiud!

PLATE 50

En blev Svin og En blev Hund
Det de var fra denne Stund.

Tre Drager og en Slange,
Og Ridderen dog ei bange.

En Hest med Næb og Vinger
Den Jomfru langtbort bringer.

One a dog, the other a boar,
Thus they were for evermore.

Three dragons and a snake
Cannot cause this knight to quake.

A horse that looks like a bird of prey
Carries the maiden far away.

The two upper pictures are entitled 'The Angry Magician Changes the Two Knights into Animals' and 'The Enchanted Forest'; the bottom picture has had its caption cropped. All come from the series noted on pl. 17.

Besides heraldic devices from various sources (see pl. 40) the small designs include the obverse and reverse sides of a Danish coin. This was minted when the Swedes, after besieging Copenhagen for some months, made a catastrophically unsuccesful assault on 11 February 1659. On one side, the enemy hand reaches for the Danish crown, only to be lopped off by the sword in God's hand ('To God alone the glory'). On the other side, the value of '4 Danish Marks 1659' is shown, with Frederik III's monogram above a biblical symbol of help — the 'Ebenezer' or stone of help (see the First Book of Samuel ch. 7 v. 12).

L'Enchanteur en courroux change les deux Chevaliers en bêtes.

La Forêt enchantée.

PLATE 51

These picture strips come from various sources: the two upper ones are German (see pl. 112), the sailing vessels are French — and the rowing boat in the combined picture at the bottom flies a French flag. The small picture in the centre and several other ships elsewhere in the book come from Danish advertisements for large and small steamboat companies. These illustrations, which vary from postage-stamp size to full column-width, often feature paddle-steamers.

PLATE 52

The first of three lithographs from volume IX of the *Düsseldorfer Monatshefte* 1857 (cf. pls 66 and 111). The printer Arnz also produced many picture-sheets, especially toy-theatre scenes. The text of the joke is as follows:

Customer: What's happened to my grilled chops?
Maid: Culés has had 'em.
Customer: Culés?
Maid: Yes, Culés.
Customer: Who's Culés?
Maid: Your dog.
Customer: But he's called Herculés.
Maid: Why should I call him 'Herr',
              when he's only a dog!

In the bottom corners are the Tivoli (see pl. 1) and a letter 'H' incorporating a picture of Hubert, the patron saint of hunting.

Lith. Jnst. v. Arnz & Cº in Düsseldorf.

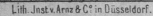

Herr. Nun wo bleibt der Schöpsenbraten.
Magd. Cules hot ihn gefreten.
Herr. Cules?
Magd. Ja Cules.
Herr. Wer ist Cules?
Magd. Jhriger Hund.
Herr. Der heist ja Hercules?
Magd. Ah wat! wer ich zu en solches Hundviech aucn noch „Herr" sagen

PLATE 53

Der er i Verden, som her Du seer,
Sommerfugl-Jagd paa forskjellig Maneer!

Look at the ways that everyone tries
To catch those fluttering butterflies.

In this elegant, hand-coloured lithograph, the little butterflies are all inscribed with more or less desirable sums of 'Reichsthaler'; the design has been taken from a Leipzig lottery prospectus. The large butterflies are more innocent, as is the combined picture below; the tree may have come from a piece of toy-theatre scenery.

PLATE 54

Hvad siger Gaardhanen Til Guldfasanen ?
Ikke noget Vigtigt, Om jeg hører rigtigt.

The barnyard cock (a bit of a peasant)
Is talking to the golden pheasant.
'What's he whispering in his ear?'
Nothing important from what I hear.

Three pheasants from the elaborate German   with insignificant pictures from other sources.
series mentioned above (pl. 5) are here combined

Der Glanzfasan.

Der Goldfasan.

Der Silberfasan.

———— PLATE 55 ————

I China spiser man Rosensylt,
Og tørrer sin Mund paa Silke-Tylt
Og saa er Eens halve Huus forgylt.

In China they make jam from roses,
Take silken cloths to wipe their noses,
And use gold paint for half their houses.

'Travellers came from all the countries of the world
to the Emperor's city and they marvelled at it, and
at the palace and the garden, but when they heard
the nightingale they all said, "Ah, but that's the
best of all!"'

'The Nightingale'
Hans Christian Andersen (1843)
(See note on pl. 41.)

PLATE 56

Den Hundeklipper
Ei dem slipper!

The poodles cannot slip away
From the poodle-clipper.

The top pictures show musical evenings in two very different environments, taken from a German magazine but drawn by two French graphic artists: Jules Worms (1832-?) and François Pierdon (1821-1904).

The lithograph below, captioned in Danish 'A Street Scene in the Dog Days', is the work of the portrait and genre painter E. Lehmann (1815-92). It reproduces a painting by the popular and respected Danish artist Wilhelm Marstrand (1810-73). The dog-catcher is unlikely to content himself with just clipping the dogs, but will prob-ably kill them — it was thought that animals were susceptible to rabies in the hot 'dog days'. The lithograph comes from Georg Carstensen's elegant weekly *Portefeuillen* for 1839 and so, like several other sheets, is twenty years older than *Christine's Picture Book.* This progressive magazine used lithography for its plates at a time when wood engravings were far more common. It specialized in art reproductions, portraits and fashion plates, together with caricatures copied from the famous French paper *Le Charivari* (see pl. 63).

PLATE 57

Stakkels Faar! hvad vilde Du der?
Ulven staaer dig altfor nær.

Bjørnen og hans Broder med Stok,
De æde Hesten imellem dem nok.

Ulven seer kjærligt til Hanen hen.
Hane vogt Dig! Flyv bort fra den Ven.

Poor old sheep, what will you do?
The wolf is creeping up on you.

The bear and his brother with the walking stick
Will eat the horse between them quick.

And now the wolf is eyeing the rooster
Watch out! His friendship's more than you're used to.

The main pictures here continue the woodcut series seen on pl. 38. As well as the easily recognizable ass, ram, bear and toucan, there is a kind of armadillo from South America and an osprey, whose peculiar Amerindian designation 'Xochitol' has been pasted over.

ANE.

TOUCAN.

BÉLIER.

KABASSOU.

OURS.

PLATE 58

Tusindbeen
Og dog seen.

Millipede
But no speed.

Of the two large German wood engravings, the upper is entitled 'Arolla Glacier on Mount Collon' (in Switzerland), the lower is probably from a piece of belles-lettres. Neither is as characteristic of Andersen as the little centre design. The much-travelled writer loved all technical progress, but especially railways, and at the end of his splendid semi-historical novella *The Wind's Story about* *Valdemar Daae and his Daughters,* published in 1859, we find these words: 'New times, different times! The old highway is submerged under enclosed fields; hallowed graves give place to busy roads, and soon the steam-engine will come with its line of carriages, roaring over graves as forgotten as those within them, hoooooh! go on ... go on ...'

Fig. 7. Der Arollagletscher am Mont Collon.

Tusindbnnn
og dog funu.

—— PLATE 59 ——

Ei hun lider Krebsegang,
Krebsene hun standser.
Otte Been af første Rang
Har hun, saa hun dandser!
Det er nydeligt at see,
Ansigt har hun, hele tre!

Backwards, crabwise,
Stop, start, stop
Her eight fine legs
Go hop, hop, hop.
Such a graceful thing to see
And look at her faces: one, two, three.

A dancer made of paper is a crucial, if silent, character in 'The Steadfast Tin Soldier', and she also appears frequently among Andersen's paper cuts. Despite the rather shabby objects she holds and the lottery tickets at her feet, this figure is unquestionably 'very fine', as stated by the label at the top of the page (which is related to the one on the title-page). This and the other Andersen cuts in the book were first published in 1961. The image of the dancer has since figured, along with other designs, as a relief on the facade of the KDD International Telecommunications Center in Tokyo, designed by the Danish architect Jan Buhl with support from the Great Northern Telegraph Company of Denmark.

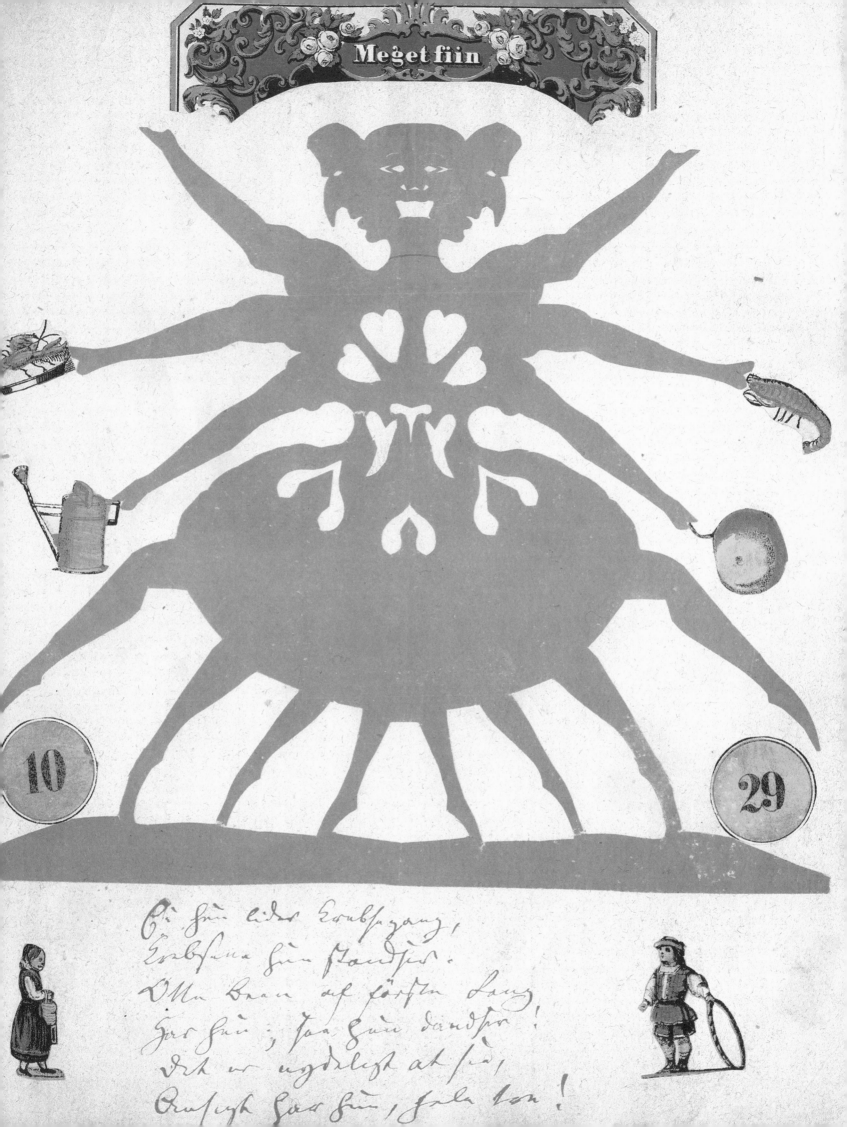

PLATE 60

Vippebrædt
Aldrig Træt!

Hunden ligestor
Med Christinemoer. —

Hundene give paa Ræven ei Agt.
Ræven løber i Jægerens Magt
Maleren var vist aldrig paa Jagt.

See-saw
For evermore.

Have you ever seen
A dog as big as Christine?

The hunter's dog don't give a damn,
The fox runs through the hunter's aim,
The artist's not a huntin' man.

These unidentified pictures are, like so many others in the book, printed by lithography and then coloured by hand. The verses attached to the hunting scene point out its curious defects: the dog is not looking at its quarry, the nearest hunter is not ready to shoot, and the one who is ready can easily be seen by the animal.

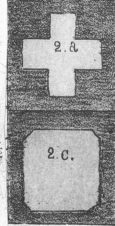

Wippebræt
Aldrig træt!

Hunden ligeslav
Und Christinemoer.

PLATE 61

Hvem løber bedst.
Blis eller Gyngehest?

Halløi!
Ingen Støi!

Vil hun skrive eller regne,
Eller troer Du, hun vil tegne?

Paa Casinos Maskerader
Vil han, som det lader.

Who gallops best around the course,
A real one or a rocking horse?

Hey there boys,
Don't make a noise!

Is she practising writing or geometry?
Or drawing something that we can't see?

It looks as though he's had it made
For a Casino masquerade.

The upper picture comes from a German leaflet or prospectus about a book published in 1855. The subject is a famous experiment carried out by the Mayor of Magdeburg, Otto von Guericke, in 1654. The inventor of a vacuum pump, he demonstrated that two teams of eight horses had the greatest difficulty in separating two halves of a sphere from which the air had been evacuated.

The bottom landscape, with its churches and mosques, seems to be oriental (but see pl. 87), and Professor Mogens Krustrup of Copenhagen suggests that the location may be Armenia or Persia. A similar little picture on pl. 20 showing a dilapidated caravanserai may be from the same part of the world. The pictures have not been traced to any particular magazine, but buildings in, and views of, exotic places were often subjects for short articles written to fill up a specific amount of space.

PLATE 62

Om disse to man seer og veed,
De mødes ei i Kjærlighed!

From this picture you may see
That lions and horses don't agree!

Similar pictures of animal ferocity are to be found
on pl. 15.

Om disse to man feer og vaad,
Du maaskee i Gedelsfud!

—— PLATE 63 ——

Hvor han er sød — den lille Engel!
Hvor han ligner sin Fader, den Bengel!

Confirmanten frygter at
Regnen skade skal hans Hat.

Moppe i den vaade Eng
Længes efter varme Seng.

Little angel, isn't he sweet!
Just like his father, little brute!

In Sunday best he's frightened that
The rain will spoil his nice new hat.

Puggy in the wet lane
Wants his cosy bed again.

The upper caricature is from the Danish *Figaro, Journal for Literatur, Kunst og Musik*, a fashionable magazine edited by Georg Carstensen. It is from the volume for 1841, copied from the Parisian *Le Charivari*, and was printed by the well-known lithographic house of Emil Bærentzen & Co, the third oldest in Copenhagen, founded in 1837. Bærentzen (1799-1868) was a painter who studied lithography in Paris in 1831-2. The printed caption to the picture seems to have inspired the manu-script line with its clinching rhyme (not entirely reflected in the English translation; 'Bengel' means 'rascal').

The lower picture 'Rainy Weather at Dyre-haven' (near Copenhagen) has an alternative title: 'The Family in the Wood'. Lithographed after the best-known painting by the young Emil Andersen (1817-45), it comes from another Carstensen magazine, the twenty-year-old *Portefeuillen* of 1839 (see pl. 56).

Hvor han er söd _ den lille Engel!

PLATE 64

Riders of all kinds were a popular subject for picture-sheets, and there are many examples to be found in *Christine's Picture Book* (e.g. pl. 102). The vertical design in the centre may be part of the wings of a marionette theatre. Backdrops, wings and the characters designed for such theatres figured largely in popular picture prints during this period when there was great interest in the stage, though most were too large to be used here.

PLATE 65

'And now the dung beetle was in a pretty little flower garden, fragrant with roses and lavender. "Isn't it charming here !" said one of the small lady-birds who were flying about with black spots on those red wings of theirs that look like tiny shields. "Lovely scent ... really beautiful ... !"

"I'm used to better things than this", said the dung beetle. "D'you call this beautiful? Why, you haven't even got a dung-heap!"'

'The Dung Beetle'
Hans Christian Andersen (1861)

PLATE 66

The second of three lithographs in the book from the *Düsseldorfer Monatshefte* (see also pls 52 and 111). The text reads: 'Well, Sally, what d'you think of *Ariadne on Naxos?*' 'What? Oh, Ariadne was all right, but I didn't care for Naxos.' This probably refers to the opera by G. Benda (1775). Several of the small pictures can be met with elsewhere in the book (e.g. pl. 43); woodcuts of pieces of furniture were used repeatedly in newspaper advertisements. 'Providentia' is a symbol frequently used in the advertisements of a Frankfurt-am-Main insurance company. The beehive is the trade mark of a Danish savings-bank; it was new at the time and is still used today.

Lith. Jnst. v Arnz & Cº in Düsseldorf.

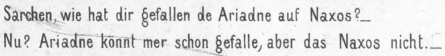

Sarchen, wie hat dir gefallen de Ariadne auf Naxos? —
Nu? Ariadne könnt mer schon gefalle, aber das Naxos nicht. —

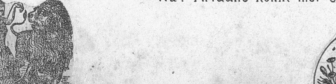

PLATE 67

Bonden gaaer bag Ploven,
Christine gaaer ind i Skoven;
Bonden vi meget godt kunme see!
Christine har skjult sig — bag Træet, kanskee!

The ploughman ploughs a steady course,
Christine comes out to see;
The ploughman's view is mostly horse,
Where's Christine? — Hiding round that tree.

A 'philosophical' question: if you draw or photograph a tree with a person hiding behind it, is that
person in the picture?

London gaaer bag Klosen,
Christian gaaer ud i Klosen;
Vorden vi maget godt Ennden se!
Christian har Skult sig — bag troed, Tanken!

PLATE 68

Amagertorv is a little square in the oldest part of Copenhagen and is here used as the title of an amazing mixture of little scenes, people, objects and advertisement lettering. In similar style, pl. 99 suggests the dire effects of a comet that has come too close to the earth: a confused assortment of bits of paper from various sources that is almost surrealist in character.

'Kometen' is also the title of one of Andersen's later, and less important, stories. It was written in 1869, and may have been inspired by Halley's comet which appeared in 1835 and 1910, and is due to be seen again in 1986.

'And the comet came, with its shining heart of flame and its threatening birch-rod of a tail. They watched it from palaces and from hovels, the crowds in the streets, and the wanderer on the trackless moors; and everyone pondered on it.'

But the Amagertorv is varied enough in itself without any comets. The symbol of the sun ('comet head') used on this plate and elsewhere should comfort rather than alarm, since it is the trade symbol of the London insurance company, the Sun Fire Office, which used to advertise in the Danish *Dagbladet* and in the *Berlingske Tidende*.

PLATE 69

Betragt
En rigtig Jagt
Midt i Africas Pragt.
— Paa Vers er det sagt.

Behold
These huntsmen bold
In Africa's burning gold —
And so poetically told!

The writer of the verses here takes poetic licence:
the scene is Indian and not African.

PLATE 70

PLATE 71

The joker ('Twang! Beware! He'll make a fool of you!') comes from a letterpress Neu Ruppin sheet, coloured by stencil and issued by the main agent Gustav Kühn: Danish no. 194, 1851-54 (in the V.E.Clausen Collection in Copenhagen). The sheet portrays a whole pack of cards, too small and flimsy to play with, which were used for fortune-telling, along with their short accompanying texts. The sheet's title was *The Old Sybil: The Art of Reading the Cards*.

The little figures, the tree and the church are a composite group; the last two may well be from a theatre sheet.

Lirum! forvar Dig!

Han holder for Nar Dig!

PLATE 72

Riis og Bog
gjør Drengen klog.

Birch and book shall
Teach the boy well.

The two large German wood engravings, with related motifs, come from a periodical; the lower one has a novella by Theodor König on its reverse side, dating from 1857. The artist ('J.R.') has not been traced and nothing is known of the engraver, C. Deuerling.

Liis og bog
gjør Drengen glad.

G.DEUERLING. SC.

PLATE 73

Madammen rider i Boutik,
det gjorde hun ei, ifald hun gik!
H.C. Andersen

Du seer hvordan en pyntet Een
Kan falde i en Rendesteen.

The lady is riding into the shop.
No she isn't, she is going to walk.
H.C. Andersen

This well-dressed fellow, walking out,
Is falling under a water-spout.

The lady rider, the student and the young couple are probably French, the first picture being signed by the Parisian illustrator Eugène Laville (1814-69). There is much play with letters and words on this page: instead of the 'o' of 'école', the Norwegian name Ola is inserted, and the seemingly loving affirmatives above and below the young couple are French (or Spanish) and German (or Danish). 'Sur' means 'for sure' in French, but in Danish it means 'sour'.

The two German printed doggerel verses read divergent but not incompatible morals into the humble occupations of farriery and fishing, while the centre picture reminds us that family reading was a custom of the period. The latter is printed on fairly thick paper, but has another picture on the reverse side.

SI

IA-

SUR

EC OLA LE

Du zur Arbeit grade Muth,
schnell daran, so wird sie gut.
Dir was ein, so schreib es auf
eiß das Eisen, hämmre drauf!

Ziehst Du zu früh die Angel an,
Kein Fischlein beißt sich fest daran;
Drum hab' Geduld zu jeder Zeit,
Wer sicher geht, kommt sicher weit.

PLATE 74

See hun er rigtig 'født' og 'baaret',
Hun kom af Æget med Kam i Haaret.

Properly born, properly bred,
Came out of the egg with a comb in her head.

34. Le Coq de roche. 35. Le Roi des Gobe-mouches

PLATE 75

Nothing is known about these lithographs, which have been hand-coloured prior to sale; but the theme of a bear-hunt suggests that they may be from a children's story.

PLATE 76

More amusing pictures based on Parisian street names (see pl. 47), including 'Sideboard Street' and 'The Washerwoman's Cul-de-Sac'. 'Battoir' can mean both a fist and a flail. The printed Danish comment stuck over the Rue du Battoir drawing reads 'Prompt and accurate service'.

Rue de la Buvette.

Rue des Bons Enfants.

Rue des Batailles.

besörges hurtigt og nöiagtigt

Impasse des Blanchisseuses.

Rue du Battoir.

PLATE 77

Moses, som Lille, fra Nilens Vand
Førtes og blev til en holden Mand,
Han døde paa Hjørnet af Canaans Land.

Picked from the Nile (when young) by hand,
Moses became a well-to-do man,
But died on a corner in Canaan's land.

Five scenes from the life of Moses from an illus-trated German Bible, the *Allgemeine, Wohlfeile Bil-der-Bibel für die Katholiken ... Sterotyp-Prachtausgabe* (Leipzig 1836-7: a copy is in the City Library at Mainz). The page is amusing but not wholly respectful — 'en holden Mand' relates only to econ-omic well-being, and 'paa Hjørnet' to life on street-corners. Things get worse on pl. 86; see also pl. 121.

The signature 'Lacoste jeune' surely refers to one of the sons of the wood engraver L.C.Lacoste, Jean-Louis-Joseph (1809-66), who produced bibli-cal illustrations after drawings by T.Johannot in 1843; but the frames are signed 'Odard'. The pic-tures may come from a French Bible; framed illustrations of this kind in Bibles and other books date back to the sixteenth century.

d, Jun Lille, fra Nilens Vand
 d, og Ven til en Galeher Mand
  dade ja, gan Hjornet af Canaans Land

PLATE 78

TRUMPFer han sender,
Men Bladet sig vender.

Bawling ... rage ...
Turn over the page.

'Concordia' and 'Trumpf' (which can mean 'oath' or 'outburst' as well as a strong card) are the headings to this set of angry scenes. The top one is German, the two at the bottom from the *Almanach Pour Rire* for 1856, with wood engravings by 'Cham' (Amédée de Noé, 1819-79). The first was also repeated for publicity purposes in *Le Charivari* for 18 December, 1855. The number added above the picture of the newly-married couple ('A chilly start') may be meant to suggest the basis of the marriage. 'Meer' at this period could have meant 'a lazy woman' in Danish but 'sea' in German, and the word has probably been taken from a German journal, perhaps *Über Land und Meer*.

Dans une mauvaise lune.

DEUX MARIÉS. — Froid précoce.

PLATE 79

Hammershuus on the rocky island of Bornholm is Denmark's largest ruin, dating from the thirteenth century; Viborg is the old administrative centre and cathedral town in Jutland. Famous as they are, neither had any particular significance for Andersen. The pictures are signed by the landscape painter Ferdinand Richardt (1819-95) and come from an advertising pamphlet put out by the well-known lithographic firm of Kittendorff & Aagaard (see pl. 35). The artist is known for his paintings, lithographs and other pictures of manor houses. Surprisingly, the Danish Royal Library has no copy or record of a pamphlet or print of this kind. However, they do have a tinted lithograph after Richardt's painting of Hammershuus, a model for the one used here.

The pictures are technically interesting in that they are not lithographs. They appear to be reproduced by the process known as chemitype, which was invented by the Dane, Christian Piil, in 1845 and used, with or without modification, in many other countries. The process involves treating an etched zinc plate in such a way that the required image appears as a raised surface which will print alongside a letterpress text, as can be seen here in the printed captions to the pictures. See pl. 121.

Richardt.

Ruiner af Hammershuus.

Richardt.

Prospect af Viborg.

PLATE 80

Naar Mennesket paa Skyen bygger,
Som en Phantast,
Han let i Stumper og i Stykker
Gaaer, og i Hast!

Storken henter Børn af Vandet,
Svanerne synge om Evigheds Landet.

H.C. Andersen fecit.

Building castles in the air,
That's what dreamers do;
They fall in bits and pieces there
And quickly too!

The storks bring
Children out of the stream.
The swans sing
Of a land of eternal dream.

H.C. Andersen fecit.

The top picture of the statue of Dionysus from the Parthenon comes from a German prospectus. With the help of a much-used decorative border, the composition forms a triangle that points downward to one of Andersen's finest silhouettes. The shapes are delicate and quite distinct, and pen lines have been added, including the charming detail of a snake in one of the herons' beaks. The importance of swans in Andersen's imagery has already been mentioned (cf. 'The Ugly Duckling'), while storks, symbolic birds of passage, appear in stories like 'The Storks' and 'The Marsh King's Daughter', and are mentioned many times in his other writings.

An der Eggen-Mühle bei Culm am 30. Aug. 1813.

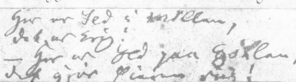

PLATE 93

An effective juxtaposition of different human types. The picture of Princess Augusta of Prussia (1811-90) probably comes from the article mentioned on pl. 8. She was the sister of the Duke of Saxony-Weimar-Eisenach, and married the man who was later to become Kaiser Wilhelm I. Andersen mentions her in his diary, and round about the New Year of 1846 had three audiences with her, read her some of his stories and received an album from her. This has been preserved and is now to be seen in the huge folio-facsimile edition of the *Hans Christian Andersen Album I–V* (Copenhagen, 1980).

The Sultan of Mayotte is a somewhat different character. Adrian-Souli came from Madagascar and conquered Mayotte on the east coast of Africa in 1831, before the French occupied it in 1841. The picture, from a German periodical, has an exact counterpart in the *Magasin Pittoresque* for June 1855, from which it may have been drawn. The magazine contains several articles about the islands of the Indian Ocean.

Auguste, Prinzessin von Preußen.

Adrian-Souli, der alte Sultan von Mayotte.

Das Orakel zu Delphi.

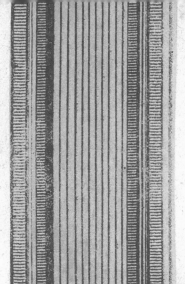

Rue des grands Plumets.

Rue de Bondy.

PLATE 94

(see previous page)

Søde Mand, det er mig en Pine,
At vi aldrig har hilst paa lille Christine!

Dearest husband, how sorry I've been
Not to have called on little Christine!

The centre picture comes from the *Berliner illu-strirte Blätter; Unterhaltungsbibliothek für Leser aller Stände* ('The Berlin Illustrated Papers; an enter-taining library for readers of all classes'). Top left is a German picture with an advertisement for popu-lar books of 1846 on its reverse side; it is signed by the Leipzig firm of wood engravers J.G. Flegel. The two pictures at the bottom are from the French series of illustrated street names first met with on pl. 47. The decorative centre strip is probably part of a toy theatre.   For reasons that are not all clear, a large picture has been added to the left hand page. It shows the Oracle at Delphi and is signed by Heinrich Leutemann (1824-1905), who drew for popular journals. The illustration, no. 359 of the splendid wood-engraved *Münchner Bilderbogen*, is the sixth in a series called 'Pictures from Antiquity' and is titled 'Greece in the time of the republics'. Like most picture-sheets, the *Bilderbogen* could be bought plain or coloured. The latter were generally more impressive than this example, which sug-gests that the colouring here is not original. The sheet is probably from 1863 and thus a later addition to the book.

PLATE 95

Koen gaaer i Vand,
Som den var en And.

A cow takes to the water
Just like the old duck's daughter.

—————————— PLATE 96 ——————————

Petits! Petits! Petits!
Putte! sige vi.

Petits! Petits! Petits!
Chickens! say we.

See pl. 9. At the foot of this continuing series of pictures of French rural activities there has been pasted a very narrow strip printed by the litho- grapher Sivertsen (see pl. 19). The writer of the Danish is making a pun on the printed text. 'Putte' means 'chickens' or 'chickies'.

Petits! Petits! Petits!

Femmes faisant des fromages.

Putte' søgn mi.

Les moissonneurs.

Le blé mis en gerbes.

La servante au puits.

Le vanneur de blé.

PLATE 97

St Nicholas, a semi-legendary figure who is said to have lived around 300 AD, is the patron saint of children, seafarers and bakers (observe the loaves). This large print seems to have been part of a prospectus for a work on the saint published in Stuttgart. As is so often the case in *Christine's Picture Book*, a picture has been supplemented with awkward small figures.

PLATE 99

(see two pages on)

Her seer Du Cometen, den har stødt paa,
Derved har den mistet sin lange Hale,
Saa Alting er væltet, kun to seer Du staae
Paa Torvet og der om Ulykken tale,
Een sidder paa Taget og skriver det op
Men Posten skynder sig hurtigst fra Byen;
Selv Ræven er bange for Skind og for Krop,
Han seer mod Cometen, der øverst bag Skyen.
Det er en Forstyrrelse — Alt er smidt om,
— det var før Christine til Verden kom!

Here is a comet that's had a collision,
Its streaming tail was gone in a flash;
And those two gents in all the confusion
Chat in the market about the crash.
Up on the roof a reporter is writing,
The diligence hurries out of the town;
Even the fox is dreadfully frightened,
Watching the comet as clouds come down.
Everything's upset, tumbled and hurled,
And all before Christine came into the world.

See the corresponding scene on pl. 68.

Der heil. Nikolaus.

PLATE 98

Det er Nutids Jupiter
Med Cigar. Ham seer I her.
Ørnen bærer Lyn i Klo,
Jupiter har røde Sko.
Engle med og uden Vinge
Maae Aviser til ham bringe.

Here's the modern Jupiter,
Just look at him with his cigar.
Lightning in the eagle's claws
(And Jupiter wears red shoes).
Winged and wingless, cutting capers,
Angels bring him all the papers.

This man standing on one of the frequently used pictures of an eagle (taken from an advertisement) is a modern rather than a classical figure — and a somewhat vulgar fellow as the verse suggests.

The landscape below is a good example of the care that went into *Christine's Picture Book:* it is made up of two trees, two birds, a milking scene and a donkey, all linked together by the background use of water-colour.

Volksjustiz in New-York.

PLATE 100

Af Kurven ta'er hun en Kage.
Christine! hvor den skal smage.

Med lidt Tørklde paa
Kunde det vist ogsaa gaae.

She's taking a cake out of the basket.
Christine, wouldn't you like to taste it?

You really would look better by half
In some sort of little scarf.

Some lively little scenes of different kinds, repro- duced by various lithographic methods; the first (top left) may be a plate from a children's book. The verse under the picture of the two women sug- gests that the one on the right would look more decent if she wore a scarf like the one on the left — again a comment aimed at adults not children.

The lithograph in the German 'outline' style at the bottom differs from all the other pictures in the book. It seems to represent a particular medieval scene with women and children being helped over a river. The helpers have scallop shells on their dresses, symbols of James the Apostle which show that their wearer has made a pilgrimage to the church of Santiago of Compostella in north-west Spain. Information given by Dr Tue Gad of Copen- hagen suggests that the scene is probably the river Arno in Italy, not far from Lucca, at the confluence of the white and the black Arno. This was on an important pilgrim road, and an order of lay breth- ren, the Altopascio Brothers, had been established in the eleventh century to help pilgrims over the river. The source of this prettily printed picture has not been traced.

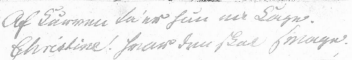

—————————— PLATE 101 ——————————

Ingen kan see paa det nøgne Skarn
Om det er Borger eller Adels Barn!
Man mærker det ei om det leer eller græder
— dog jo — det kan sees paa de tynde Klæder.

Naked — what's the difference
Between the child of tramp or prince?
Dressed — one glance at seam and stitch
And you can tell at once which one is which.

Could this young mother be Queen Victoria, whose youngest child was born in 1857, or the Empress Elisabeth of Austria, whose first two children were born in 1856 and 1858? The picture comes from F.W. Bader's well-known art-engraving shop in Vienna, but the artist's signature is less certain. It is most likely Gottfried Kühn who worked in Leipzig from 1852 as a draughtsman preparing work for the wood engravers. His customers were often journal publishers, but there is no evidence of this on the reverse of the picture.

The promontory and lighthouse on the Kertsch peninsula had been in the news a few years earlier, when the town of that name was destroyed by shelling in the Crimean War (the place made news for the same reasons in the Second World War).

Of the small pictures, that of the wicker chair can be seen in the *Berlingske Tidende* and the *Tiden* in advertisements for 'Reiches Kurveudsalg' ('Reiche's Basket-work Shop') in Copenhagen.

Vorgebirge und Leuchtthurm auf Kertsch.

———— PLATE 102 ————

Christine paa Strudsen
Til megen Studsen
For hver Præstø Mø
Rider til Nysø.

Christine takes an ostrich
And rides to Nysø
To the great consternation
Of the girls of Præstø.

Nysø was the manor house owned by the Stampe grandparents; Præstø a nearby town. Several hand-coloured lithographs in the book show riders at various times and in various places (see pl. 64). Judging by their format, these pictures may well have come from a children's book, but it has been impossible to determine which.

PLATE 103

These two pictures are made up of four and three scraps respectively. The caption to the upper one is a relevant but, in this context, satirical advertiser's note from a Danish journal: 'Pointers — complete training for their use as hunting dogs'.

Hønsehundens
fuldstændige Dressur til Brug ved Jagten

PLATE 104

Gammel og graa;
Kan ei staae;
Kan ei gaae.

Fed og tyk   *Christine i Bad*
Temlig styg.   *Er saa glad. —*

Han har solgt sine Been,
Sikken En! Sikken En!

2 Heste og 1 And!
Drikke i Vand.

Old and grey;
Can't get up
Or walk away.

Big fat peasant,   Christine's bath
Rather unpleasant.   Good for a laugh.

What a clown! What a clown!
Sold his legs for half-a-crown.

Two horses and one duck
Drinking all the water up.

The bottom pictures, 'Home from the Fields' and 'Horses Drinking', continue the pastoral series from France first noted on pl. 9. Sources for the other pictures have not been traced, and the name 'William' does not seem to refer to anyone in the family circle. (See pl. 16.)

William

Snd og bly
Lemlig fryg

Christine i bad
ba saa glad. —

Saa har folgt sin benn
Fabben Eu! Febben Eu!

2 Huster og 1 And!
Abben i Band.

Le retour des champs.

Les chevaux à l'abreuvoir.

DINER

du 31 Août 1858.

Potage à la Hollandaise, filets de volaille.

Melon.

Rissoles aux champignons.

Rable de daim piqué — gélée — sauce.

Turbot — 2 sauces — pommes de terre.

Poulets à la Singara — sauce aux truffes.

{ Artichauts au beurre.

{ Haricots verts — saumon fumé.

Maccaronis au gratin au parmesan.

Rôti de poules de bruyère — compote — salade.

Gelée au vin.

Gâteaux.

Glaces — méringues — biscuits.

Dessert.

St. Julien.

Port. & Madère.

Romanée.

Steinwein.

Château Margeaux.

Champagne.

Malvoisie Madère.

Ferslew

Pudel.

s mig fattig Mand nu
Lidta,

hat mau mig Raban
Sölta!

Af Döds Salladut levur
mau,
At Hunda og han sa'n Soufaud.

Jeg folger Saaunen i Lamn,

Hyrdehund.

Clmut yua fula Hoskun of Lamn.

———— PLATE 116 ————

Fidtelam har den Tro
Han bør hos Faarene boe.

Fidtelam bilder sig ind
Han gaaer i Faareskind.

Look at my little fat lamb,
Wants to live in a sheep-pen.

My fat lamb, look at him,
Wants to wear a sheep-skin.

'Fidtelam' does mean 'fat lamb' in Danish, but it has human overtones in that it refers to a game, indicated here by the two figures at the left hand end of the second picture: the big boy runs round with the small boy on his back, asking people if they want to buy his little fat lamb.

Fürtalaus fear den Foro,
Han bör hos Jauruua bor.

Fürtalaus bielder fig ud,
Han gaaur i Jaauufrud.

———— PLATE 117 ————

Ulve, tag Jer iagt! — En Snare er Jer lagt! Vær paa
Vagt! paa Vagt!

Wolves, wolves, beware!
That thing is a snare!
Wolves, take care, take care!

These hunting pictures are part of the group shown on pl. 69. The animal on the cart is a tame hunting leopard which has been chained up. The lower picture seems to be a misunderstanding; it portrays a method of catching or killing animals, even people, by strangling them in a noose tied to springy branches (see that unpleasant story in the Grimm collection 'The Wonderful Musician'). But if the wolves in this picture were to jump up to get the bait in the bowl they would hit the two branches and the whole thing would fall over; there is no sign of a noose. Information on the hunting scenes has been supplied by Count Ahlefeldt-Laurvig-Bille of Egeskov Manor.

PLATE 118

Kysses vil disse,
Tilvisse!

Anden gjerne
Vil sig fjerne.

Is this
A loving kiss?

Some would rather
Move off farther.

Vautour.

PLATE 119

Kongeørnen vil
Til Christinelil!
Ballonen ligesaa.
Bare det vil gaae!

Solen vil han ta'e —
Ha! ha! ha! ha!
Sommerfuglen vil
See lidt paa det Spil.

Om de stønne skal de staae,
Maae ei til hinanden gaae.

Saagjerne han vilde
den Sommerfugl drille!

Saadan kan han rende
Til Verdens Ende.

The golden eagle
And the big balloon
Are going to Christine's
For the afternoon.

Monkey wants the sun —
Oh! what fun!
These butterflies came
To enjoy the game.

With groans they stand apart forever,
They shall never come together.

Butterfly teasing
Is very pleasing.

Running for all he's worth
To the very ends of the earth.

People and animals have been added to this strange neogothic object with a cross on its inner wall; its function cannot be easily determined as it probably formed the upper part of a larger whole.

PLATE 120

Den liden Fyr
Skal holde Styr
Paa storen Tyr.

Faaret vil
Dog see til
Paa det Spil.

Hvorom tale disse to ?
Om Christine, kan Du troe.

Lammet vil have den Ko
Til at lege Tagfat — Jo, jo!
Hun holder af Ro,
Vil ligge og gloe.
Ho, ho! Ho, ho!

The little chap
Has the job
Of looking after the bull.

The sheep will
Watch till
They find him playing the fool.

What are these two talking about?
Little Christine, without a doubt.

Lamb wants cow
To play tag — ow, ow!
She wants to lie there
And do nothing but chew and stare,
Ho! Ho! Ho!

For the cow standing centre left, see pl. 16.

PLATE 121

Again a religious element is introduced: 'Then spake Joshua to the Lord in the day when the Lord delivered up the Amorites before the children of Israel, and he said in the sight of Israel, "Sun, stand thou still upon Gibeon; and thou Moon, in the valley of Ajalon."' (Book of Joshua, Ch. X). This upper print is from the German picture Bible noted above on pls 77 and 86, in which it is immediately followed by the little picture on pl. 43.

The bottom print is a Descent from the Cross after the Bolognese painter Annibale Caracci (1560-1609). The signature to this print states that it is printed in relief (i.e. by a letterpress method) although it looks more like an intaglio steel engraving. An investigation by Poul Steen Larsen confirms that it is indeed a relief print, using a method similar to Piil's chemitype process (see pl. 79). This is the so-called 'chalkotype', invented or adapted by Heinrich Heims, who lived in Paris from 1854-8 but launched the new technique in Berlin in 1851 with an advertisement for his 'Chalkotypisches Institut'. This advertisement is reproduced in Konrad Bauer's *Aventur und Kunst* published by the Bauersche Giesserei (Frankfurt, 1940). It so happens Heims was born at Altona in Holstein in 1817 as a Danish citizen, and trained as a painter and engraver on copper in Copenhagen.

Peint par Annibal Carraci.

Prod. en relief par H. Heims.

PLATE 122

Til den gaaer under
Er lange Stunder.

Den kaprer den Seiler
Om jeg ei feiler.

It's a long, long time
Till the ship goes down.

That ship will be taken
If I'm not mistaken.

The right-hand half of the bottom picture is a combination of a ship from a Danish newspaper and a wave from a German one.

The book ends with a little picture pasted on to the verso of this leaf showing a drover on a bridge (although the Danish 'Driver' can also mean 'a lazy person') — an inhabitant of Copenhagen, far removed both from the book's diverse fantasy world, and from little Christine's everyday horizons.

En Driver.
(Nr. 2.)

Paa Broen.

POSTSCRIPT

"Godfather could tell stories – lots of them, and long ones too! What's more he could draw pictures and he could cut out pictures, and when Christmas was coming he would get hold of a writing-book with plain white pages and he'd paste the pictures into it that he'd cut out of books and newspapers; and if he couldn't find enough to suit his story then he'd draw them himself. When I was little I used to get lots of picture books like that but the nicest of them all was the one about 'that amazing year when Copenhagen got gas-lamps instead of the old oil ones' – that's what it said on the very first page.

'You must look after that book very carefully,' said Mother and Father, 'it can only come out on high days and holidays!' But Godfather had written this on the binding:-

> If the book gets torn don't worry or fret,
>
> Other little friends here have done worse yet.

Best of all was when Godfather himself looked at the book with me, read the verses and the things written there, and told me lots else besides; then the story really was a story."

Hans Christian Andersen's 'Gudfaders Billedbog'
(Godfather's Picture Book, 1868)